The Cat and the Birds
and Other Fables by Aesop

The British Library

This edition of selected fables first published in 2014 by
The British Library
96 Euston Road
London NW1 2DB

V. S. Vernon Jones's translation of Aesop's fables,
with illustrations by Arthur Rackham, was originally
published in 1912 by Heinemann

British Library Cataloguing in Publication Data
A CIP Record for this book is available from
The British Library

ISBN 978 0 7123 5722 7

Designed by Tony Antoniou,
British Library Design Office

Printed and bound in Hong Kong by Great Wall
Printing Co. Ltd

Contents

The Hound and the Hare

A young hound started a hare, and, when he caught her up, would at one moment snap at her with his teeth as though he were about to kill her, while at another he would let go his hold and frisk about her, as if he were playing with another dog. At last the hare said, 'I wish you would show yourself in your true colours! If you are my friend, why do you bite me? If you are my enemy, why do you play with me?'

He is no friend who plays double.

The Goose that Laid the Golden Eggs

A man and his wife had the good fortune to possess a goose which laid a golden egg every day. Lucky though they were, they soon began to think they were not getting rich fast enough, and, imagining the bird must be made of gold inside, they decided to kill it in order to secure the whole store of precious metal at once. But when they cut it open they found it was just like any other goose. Thus, they neither got rich all at once, as they had hoped, nor enjoyed any longer the daily addition to their wealth.

Much wants more and loses all.

The Lion and the Boar

One hot and thirsty day in the height of summer a lion and a boar came down to a little spring at the same moment to drink. In a trice they were quarrelling as to who should drink first. The quarrel soon became a fight and they attacked one another with the utmost fury. Presently, stopping for a moment to take breath, they saw some vultures seated on a rock above evidently waiting for one of them to be killed, when they would fly down and feed upon the carcase. The sight sobered them at once, and they made up their quarrel, saying, 'We had much better be friends than fight and be eaten by vultures'.

The Heifer and the Ox

A heifer went up to an ox, who was straining hard at the plough, and sympathised with him in a rather patronising sort of way on the necessity of his having to work so hard. Not long afterwards there was a festival in the village and every one kept holiday: but, whereas the ox was turned loose into the pasture, the heifer was seized and led off to sacrifice. 'Ah', said the ox, with a grim smile, 'I see now why you were allowed to have such an idle time: it was because you were always intended for the altar'.

The Fox and the Stork

A fox invited a stork to dinner, at which the only fare provided was a large flat dish of soup. The fox lapped it up with great relish, but the stork with her long bill tried in vain to partake of the savoury broth. Her evident distress caused the sly fox much amusement. But not long after the stork invited him in turn, and set before him a pitcher with a long and narrow neck, into which she could get her bill with ease. Thus, while she enjoyed her dinner, the fox sat by hungry and helpless, for it was impossible for him to reach the tempting contents of the vessel.

The Peacock and Juno

The peacock was greatly discontented because he had not a beautiful voice like the nightingale, and he went and complained to Juno about it. 'The nightingale's song', said he, 'is the envy of all the birds; but whenever I utter a sound I become a laughing stock'. The goddess tried to console him by saying, 'You have not, it is true, the power of song, but then you far excel all the rest in beauty: your neck flashes like the emerald and your splendid tail is a marvel of gorgeous colour'. But the peacock was not appeased. 'What is the use', said he, 'of being beautiful, with a voice like mine?' Then Juno replied, with a shade of sternness in her tones, 'Fate has allotted to all their destined gifts: to yourself beauty, to the eagle strength, to the nightingale song, and so on to all the rest in their degree; but you alone are dissatisfied with your portion. Make, then, no complaints: for, if your present wish were granted, you would quickly find cause for fresh discontent'.

The Monkey as King

At a gathering of all the animals the monkey danced and delighted them so much that they made him their king. The fox, however, was very much disgusted at the promotion of the monkey: so having one day found a trap with a piece of meat in it, he took the monkey there and said to him, 'Here is a dainty morsel I have found, sire; I did not take it for myself, because I thought it ought to be reserved for you, our king. Will you be pleased to accept it?' The monkey made at once for the meat and got caught in the trap. Then he bitterly reproached the fox for leading him into danger; but the fox only laughed and said, 'O monkey, you call yourself king of the beasts and haven't more sense than to be taken in like that!'

The Ass in the Lion's Skin

An ass found a lion's skin, and dressed himself up in it. Then he went about frightening every one he met, for they all took him to be a lion, men and beasts alike, and took to their heels when they saw him coming. Elated by the success of his trick, he loudly brayed in triumph.

The fox heard him, and recognised him at once for the ass he was, and said to him, 'Oho, my friend, it's you, is it? I, too, should have been afraid if I hadn't heard your voice'.

The North Wind and the Sun

A dispute arose between the north wind and the sun, each claiming that he was stronger than the other. At last they agreed to try their powers upon a traveller, to see which could soonest strip him of his cloak. The north wind had the first try; and, gathering up all his force for the attack, he came whirling furiously down upon the man, and caught up his cloak as though he would wrest it from him by one single effort: but the harder he blew, the more closely the man wrapped it round himself. Then came the turn of the sun. At first he beamed gently upon the traveller, who soon unclasped his cloak and walked on with it hanging loosely about his shoulders: then he shone forth in his full strength, and the man, before he had gone many steps, was glad to throw his cloak right off and complete his journey more lightly clad.

Persuasion is better than force.

The Fox and the Lion

A fox who had never seen a lion one day met one, and was so terrified at the sight of him that he was ready to die with fear. After a time he met him again, and was still rather frightened, but not nearly so much as he had been when he met him first. But when he saw him for the third time he was so far from being afraid that he went up to him and began to talk to him as if he had known him all his life.

The Athenian and the Theban

An Athenian and a Theban were on the road together, and passed the time in conversation, as is the way of travellers. After discussing a variety of subjects they began to talk about heroes, a topic that tends to be more fertile than edifying. Each of them was lavish in his praises of the heroes of his own city, until eventually the Theban asserted that Hercules was the greatest hero who had ever lived on earth, and now occupied a foremost place among the gods; while the Athenian insisted that Theseus was far superior, for his fortune had been in every way supremely blessed, whereas Hercules had at one time been forced to act as a servant. And he gained his point, for he was a very glib fellow, like all Athenians; so that the Theban, who was no match for him in talking, cried at last in some disgust, 'All right, have your way; I only hope that, when our heroes are angry with us, Athens may suffer from the anger of Hercules, and Thebes only from that of Theseus'.

The Wolf and the Crane

A wolf once got a bone stuck in his throat. So he went to a crane and begged her to put her long bill down his throat and pull it out. 'I'll make it worth your while', he added. The crane did as she was asked, and got the bone out quite easily. The wolf thanked her warmly, and was just turning away, when she cried, 'What about that fee of mine?' 'Well, what about it?' snapped the wolf, baring his teeth as he spoke; 'you can go about boasting that you once put your head into a wolf's mouth and didn't get it bitten off. What more do you want?'

The Walnut-Tree

A walnut-tree, which grew by the roadside, bore every year a plentiful crop of nuts. Every one who passed by pelted its branches with sticks and stones, in order to bring down the fruit, and the tree suffered severely. 'It is hard', it cried, 'that the very persons who enjoy my fruit should thus reward me with insults and blows'.

Arthur Rackham. 1912

The Crow and the Pitcher

A thirsty crow found a pitcher with some water in it, but so little was there that, try as she might, she could not reach it with her beak, and it seemed as though she would die of thirst within sight of her remedy. At last she hit upon a clever plan. She began dropping pebbles into the pitcher, and with each pebble the water rose a little higher until at last it reached the brim, and the knowing bird was enabled to quench her thirst.

Necessity is the mother of invention.

The Fox Without a Tail

A fox once fell into a trap, and after a struggle managed to get free, but with the loss of his brush. He was then so much ashamed of his appearance that he thought life was not worth living unless he could persuade the other foxes to part with their tails also, and thus divert attention from his own loss. So he called a meeting of all the foxes, and advised them to cut off their tails: 'They're ugly things anyhow', he said, 'and besides they're heavy, and it's tiresome to be always carrying them about with you'. But one of the other foxes said, 'My friend, if you hadn't lost your own tail, you wouldn't be so keen on getting us to cut off ours'.

The Mice and the Weasels

There was war between the mice and the weasels, in which the mice always got the worst of it, numbers of them being killed and eaten by the weasels. So they called a council of war, in which an old mouse got up and said, 'It's no wonder we are always beaten, for we have no generals to plan our battles and direct our movements in the field'. Acting on his advice, they chose the biggest mice to be their leaders, and these, in order to be distinguished from the rank and file, provided themselves with helmets bearing large plumes of straw. They then led out the mice to battle, confident of victory; but they were defeated as usual, and were soon scampering as fast as they could to their holes. All made their way to safety without difficulty except the leaders, who were so hampered by the badges of their rank that they could not get into their holes, and fell easy victims to their pursuers.

Greatness carries its own penalties.

The Lion and the Wild Ass

A lion and a wild ass went out hunting together: the latter was to run down the prey by his superior speed, and the former would then come up and despatch it. They met with great success; and when it came to sharing the spoil the lion divided it all into three equal portions. 'I will take the first', said he, 'because I am king of the beasts; I will also take the second, because, as your partner, I am entitled to half of what remains; and as for the third—well, unless you give it up to me and take yourself off pretty quick, the third, believe me, will make you feel very sorry for yourself!'

Might makes right.

The Farmer, His Boy, and the Rooks

A farmer had just sown a field of wheat, and was keeping a careful watch over it, for numbers of rooks and starlings kept continually settling on it and eating up the grain. Along with him went his boy, carrying a sling: and whenever the farmer asked for the sling the starlings understood what he said and warned the rooks and they were off in a moment. So the farmer hit on a trick. 'My lad', said he, 'we must get the better of these birds somehow. After this, when I want the sling, I won't say "sling", but just "humph!" and you must then hand me the sling quickly'. Presently back came the whole flock. 'Humph!' said the farmer; but the starlings took no notice, and he had time to sling several stones among them, hitting one on the head, another in the legs, and another in the wing, before they got out of range. As they made all haste away they met some cranes, who asked them what the matter was. 'Matter?' said one of the rooks; 'it's those rascals, men, that are the matter. Don't you go near them. They have a way of saying one thing and meaning another which has just been the death of several of our poor friends'.

The Fox and the Crow

A crow was sitting on a branch of a tree with a piece of cheese in her beak when a fox observed her and set his wits to work to discover some way of getting the cheese. Coming and standing under the tree he looked up and said, 'What a noble bird I see above me! Her beauty is without equal, the hue of her plumage exquisite. If only her voice is as sweet as her looks are fair, she ought without doubt to be Queen of the Birds'. The crow was hugely flattered by this, and just to show the fox that she could sing she gave a loud caw. Down came the cheese, of course, and the fox, snatching it up, said, 'You have a voice, madam, I see: what you want is wits'.

ARackham /12

The Wolf in Sheep's Clothing

A wolf resolved to disguise himself in order that he might prey upon a flock of sheep without fear of detection. So he clothed himself in a sheepskin, and slipped among the sheep when they were out at pasture. He completely deceived the shepherd, and when the flock was penned for the night he was shut in with the rest. But that very night as it happened, the shepherd, requiring a supply of mutton for the table, laid hands on the wolf in mistake for a sheep, and killed him with his knife on the spot.

The Ass and the Dog

An ass and a dog were on their travels together, and, as they went along, they found a sealed packet lying on the ground. The ass picked it up, broke the seal, and found it contained some writing, which he proceeded to read out aloud to the dog. As he read on it turned out to be all about grass and barley and hay – in short, all the kinds of fodder that asses are fond of. The dog was a good deal bored with listening to all this, till at last his impatience got the better of him, and he cried, 'Just skip a few pages, friend, and see if there isn't something about meat and bones'. The ass glanced all through the packet, but found nothing of the sort, and said so. Then the dog said in disgust, 'Oh, throw it away, do: what's the good of a thing like that?'

The Cage-Bird and the Bat

A singing-bird was confined in a cage which hung outside a window, and had a way of singing at night when all other birds were asleep. One night a bat came and clung to the bars of the cage, and asked the bird why she was silent by day and sang only at night. 'I have a very good reason for doing so,' said the bird: 'it was once when I was singing in the daytime that a fowler was attracted by my voice, and set his nets for me and caught me. Since then I have never sung except by night'. But the bat replied, 'It is no use your doing that now when you are a prisoner: if only you had done so before you were caught, you might still have been free'.

Precautions are useless after the event.

The Frogs Asking for a King

Time was when the frogs were discontented because they had no one to rule over them: so they sent a deputation to Jupiter to ask him to give them a king. Jupiter, despising the folly of their request, cast a log into the pool where they lived, and said that that should be their king. The frogs were terrified at first by the splash, and scuttled away into the deepest parts of the pool; but by and by, when they saw that the log remained motionless, one by one they ventured to the surface again, and before long, growing bolder, they began to feel such contempt for it that they even took to sitting upon it. Thinking that a king of that sort was an insult to their dignity, they sent to Jupiter a second time, and begged him to take away the sluggish king he had given them, and to give them another and a better one. Jupiter, annoyed at being pestered in this way, sent a stork to rule over them, who no sooner arrived among them than he began to catch and eat the frogs as fast as he could.

The Kingdom of the Lion

When the lion reigned over the beasts of the earth he was never cruel or tyrannical, but as gentle and just as a king ought to be. During his reign he called a general assembly of the beasts, and drew up a code of laws under which all were to live in perfect equality and harmony: the wolf and the lamb, the tiger and the stag, the leopard and the kid, the dog and the hare, all should dwell side by side in unbroken peace and friendship. The hare said, 'Oh! how I have longed for this day when the weak take their place without fear by the side of the strong!'

The Pomegranate, the Apple-Tree, and the Bramble

A pomegranate and an apple-tree were disputing about the quality of their fruits, and each claimed that its own was the better of the two. High words passed between them, and a violent quarrel was imminent, when a bramble impudently poked its head out of a neighbouring hedge and said, 'There, that's enough, my friends: don't let us quarrel'.

The Grasshopper and the Ants

One fine day in winter some ants were busy drying their store of corn, which had got rather damp during a long spell of rain. Presently up came a grasshopper and begged them to spare her a few grains. 'For', she said, 'I'm simply starving'. The ants stopped work for a moment, though this was against their principles. 'May we ask', said they, 'what you were doing with yourself all summer? Why didn't you collect a store of food for the winter?' 'The fact is', replied the grasshopper, 'I was so busy singing that I hadn't the time'. 'If you spent the summer singing', replied the ants, 'you can't do better than spend the winter dancing'. And they chuckled and went on with their work.

The Tortoise and the Eagle

A tortoise, discontented with his lowly life, and envious of the birds he saw disporting themselves in the air, begged an eagle to teach him to fly. The eagle protested that it was idle for him to try, as nature had not provided him with wings; but the tortoise pressed him with entreaties and promises of treasure, insisting that it could only be a question of learning the craft of the air. So at length the eagle consented to do the best he could for him, and picked him up in his talons. Soaring with him to a great height in the sky he then let him go, and the wretched tortoise fell headlong and was dashed to pieces on a rock.

The Fox and the Grasshopper

A grasshopper sat chirping in the branches of a tree. A fox heard her, and, thinking what a dainty morsel she would make, he tried to get her down by a trick. Standing below in full view of her, he praised her song in the most flattering terms, and begged her to descend, saying he would like to make the acquaintance of the owner of so beautiful a voice. But she was not to be taken in, and replied, 'You are very much mistaken, my dear sir, if you imagine I am going to come down: I keep well out of the way of you and your kind ever since the day when I saw the numbers of grasshoppers' wings strewn about the entrance to a fox's earth'.

The Dog in the Manger

A dog was lying in a manger on the hay which had been put there for the cattle, and when they came and tried to eat, he growled and snapped at them and wouldn't let them get at their food. 'What a selfish beast', said one of them to his companions; 'he can't eat himself and yet he won't let those eat who can'.

The Thieves and the Cock

Some thieves broke into a house, and found nothing worth taking except a cock, which they seized and carried off with them. When they were preparing their supper, one of them caught up the cock, and was about to wring his neck, when he cried out for mercy and said, 'Pray do not kill me: you will find me a most useful bird, for I rouse honest men to their work in the morning by my crowing'. But the thief replied with some heat, 'Yes, I know you do, making it still harder for us to get a livelihood. Into the pot you go!'

The Blacksmith and His Dog

A blacksmith had a little dog, which used to sleep when his master was at work, but was very wide awake indeed when it was time for meals. One day his master pretended to be disgusted at this, and when he had thrown him a bone as usual, he said, 'What on earth is the good of a lazy cur like you? When I am hammering away at my anvil, you just curl up and go to sleep: but no sooner do I stop for a mouthful of food than you wake up and wag your tail to be fed'.

Those who will not work deserve to starve.

The Hound and the Fox

A hound, roaming in the forest, spied a lion, and being well used to lesser game, gave chase, thinking he would make a fine quarry. Presently the lion perceived that he was being pursued; so, stopping short, he rounded on his pursuer and gave a loud roar. The hound immediately turned tail and fled. A fox, seeing him running away, jeered at him and said, 'Ho! ho! There goes the coward who chased a lion and ran away the moment he roared!'

The Fox and the Grapes

A hungry fox saw some fine bunches of grapes hanging from a vine that was trained along a high trellis, and did his best to reach them by jumping as high as he could into the air. But it was all in vain, for they were just out of reach: so he gave up trying, and walked away with an air of dignity and unconcern, remarking, 'I thought those grapes were ripe, but I see now they are quite sour'.

The Lion, the Mouse, and the Fox

A lion was lying asleep at the mouth of his den when a mouse ran over his back and tickled him so that he woke up with a start and began looking about him everywhere to see what it was that had disturbed him. A fox, who was looking on, thought he would have a joke at the expense of the lion; so he said, 'Well this is the first time I've seen a lion afraid of a mouse'. 'Afraid of a mouse?' said the lion testily; 'not I! It's his bad manners I can't stand'.

The Dogs and the Hides

Once upon a time a number of dogs, who were famished with hunger, saw some hides steeping in a river, but couldn't get at them because the water was too deep. So they put their heads together, and decided to drink away at the river till it was shallow enough for them to reach the hides. But long before that happened they burst themselves with drinking.

The Frogs and the Well

Two frogs lived together in a marsh. But one hot summer the marsh dried up, and they left it to look for another place to live in: for frogs like damp places if they can get them. By and by they came to a deep well, and one of them looked down into it, and said to the other, 'This looks a nice cool place: let us jump in and settle here'. But the other, who had a wiser head on his shoulders, replied, 'Not so fast, my friend: supposing this well dried up like the marsh, how should we get out again?'

Think twice before you act.

The Rich Man and the Tanner

A rich man took up his residence next door to a tanner, and found the smell of the tan-yard so extremely unpleasant that he told him he must go. The tanner delayed his departure, and the rich man had to speak to him several times about it; and every time the tanner said he was making arrangements to move very shortly. This went on for some time, till at last the rich man got so used to the smell that he ceased to mind it, and troubled the tanner with his objections no more.

The Eagle and His Captor

A man once caught an eagle, and after clipping his wings turned him loose among the fowls in his hen-house, where he moped in a corner, looking very dejected and forlorn. After a while his captor was glad enough to sell him to a neighbour, who took him home and let his wings grow again. As soon as he had recovered the use of them, the eagle flew out and caught a hare, which he brought home and presented to his benefactor. A fox observed this, and said to the eagle, 'Don't waste your gifts on him! Go and give them to the man who first caught you; make him your friend, and then perhaps he won't catch you and clip your wings a second time'.

The Kid and the Wolf

A kid strayed from the flock and was chased by a wolf. When he saw he must be caught he turned round and said to the wolf, 'I know, sir, that I can't escape being eaten by you: and so, as my life is bound to be short, I pray that you let it be as merry as may be. Will you not play me a tune to dance to before I die?' The wolf saw no objection to having some music before his dinner: so he took out his pipe and began to play, while the kid danced before him. Before many minutes were passed the gods who guarded the flock heard the sound and came up to see what was going on. They no sooner clapped eyes on the wolf than they gave chase and drove him away. As he ran off, he turned and said to the kid, 'It's what I thoroughly deserve: my trade is the butcher's, and I had no business to turn piper to please you'.

The Mistress and Her Servants

A widow, thrifty and industrious, had two servants, whom she kept pretty hard at work. They were not allowed to lie long abed in the mornings, but the old lady had them up and doing as soon as the cock crew. They disliked intensely having to get up at such an hour, especially in winter-time: and they thought that if it were not for the cock waking up their mistress so horribly early, they could sleep longer. So they caught it and wrung its neck. But they weren't prepared for the consequences. For what happened was that their mistress, not hearing the cock crow as usual, waked them up earlier than ever, and set them to work in the middle of the night.

The Miller, His Son, and Their Ass

A miller, accompanied by his young son, was driving his ass to market in the hopes of finding a purchaser for him. On the road they met a troop of girls, laughing and talking, who exclaimed, 'Did you ever see such a pair of fools? To be trudging along the dusty road when they might be riding!' The miller thought there was sense in what they said; so he made his son mount the ass, and himself walked at the side. Presently they met some of his old cronies, who greeted them and said, 'You'll spoil that son of yours, letting him ride while you toil along on foot! Make him walk, young lazybones! It'll do him all the good in the world'. The miller followed their advice, and took his son's place on the back of the ass while the boy trudged along behind. They had not gone far when they overtook a party of women and children, and the miller heard them say, 'What a selfish old man! He himself rides in comfort, but lets his poor little boy follow as best he can on his own legs!' So he made his son get up behind him. Further along the road they met some travellers, who asked the miller whether the ass he was riding was his own property, or a beast hired for the occasion. He replied that it was his own, and that he was taking it to market to sell. 'Good heavens!' said they, 'with a load like that the poor beast will be so exhausted by the time he gets there that no one will look at him. Why, you'd do better to carry him!' 'Anything to please you', said the old man, 'we can but try'. So they got off, tied the ass's legs together with a rope and slung him on a pole, and at last reached the town, carrying him between them. This was so absurd a sight that the people ran out in crowds to laugh at it, and chaffed the father and son unmercifully, some even calling them lunatics. They had got them to a bridge over the river, where the ass, frightened by the noise and his unusual situation, kicked and struggled till he broke the ropes that bound him, and fell into the water and was drowned. Whereupon the unfortunate miller, vexed and ashamed, made the best of his way home again, convinced that in trying to please all he had pleased none, and had lost his ass into the bargain.

The Stag at the Pool

A thirsty stag went down to a pool to drink. As he bent over the surface he saw his own reflection in the water, and was struck with admiration for his fine spreading antlers, but at the same time he felt nothing but disgust for the weakness and slenderness of his legs. While he stood there looking at himself, he was seen and attacked by a lion; but in the chase which ensued, he soon drew away from his pursuer, and kept his lead as long as the ground over which he ran was open and free of trees. But coming presently to a wood, he was caught by his antlers in the branches, and fell a victim to the teeth and claws of his enemy. 'Woe is me!', he cried with his last breath; 'I despised my legs, which might have saved my life: but I gloried in my horns, and they have proved my ruin'.

What is worth most is often valued least.

The Two Soldiers and the Robber

Two soldiers travelling together were set upon by a robber. One of them ran away, but the other stood his ground, and laid about him so lustily with his sword that the robber was fain to fly and leave him in peace. When the coast was clear the timid one ran back, and, flourishing his weapon, cried in a threatening voice, 'Where is he? Let me get at him, and I'll soon let him know whom he's got to deal with'. But the other replied, 'You are a little late, my friend: I only wish you had backed me up just now, even if you had done no more than speak, for I should have been encouraged, believing your words to be true. As it is, calm yourself, and put up your sword: there is no further use for it. You may delude others into thinking you're as brave as a lion: but I know that, at the first sign of danger, you run away like a hare'.

The Ass and the Old Peasant

An old peasant was sitting in a meadow watching his ass, which was grazing close by, when all of a sudden he caught sight of armed men stealthily approaching. He jumped up in a moment, and begged the ass to fly with him as fast as he could, 'Or else', said he, 'we shall both be captured by the enemy'. But the ass just looked round lazily and said, 'And if so, do you think they'll make me carry heavier loads than I have to now?' 'No', said his master. 'Oh, well then', said the ass, 'I don't mind if they do take me, for I shan't be any worse off'.

The Monkey and the Dolphin

When people go on a voyage they often take with them lap-dogs or monkeys as pets to wile away the time. Thus it fell out that a man returning to Athens from the East had a pet monkey on board with him. As they neared the coast of Attica a great storm burst upon them, and the ship capsized. All on board were thrown into the water, and tried to save themselves by swimming, the monkey among the rest. A dolphin saw him, and, supposing him to be a man, took him on his back and began swimming towards the shore. When they got near Piraeus, which is the port of Athens, the

dolphin asked the monkey if he was an Athenian. The monkey replied that he was, and added that he came of a very distinguished family. 'Then, of course, you know Piraeus', continued the dolphin. The monkey thought he was referring to some high official or other, and replied, 'Oh, yes, he's a very old friend of mine'. At that, detecting his hypocrisy, the dolphin was so disgusted that he dived below the surface, and the unfortunate monkey was quickly drowned.

The Herdsman and the Lost Bull

A herdsman was tending his cattle when he missed a young bull, one of the finest of the herd. He went at once to look for him, but, meeting with no success in his search, he made a vow that, if he should discover the thief, he would sacrifice a calf to Jupiter. Continuing his search, he entered a thicket, where he presently espied a lion devouring the lost bull. Terrified with fear, he raised his hands to heaven and cried, 'Great Jupiter, I vowed I would sacrifice a calf to thee if I should discover the thief: but now a full-grown bull I promise thee if only I myself escape unhurt from his clutches'.

The Debtor and His Sow

A man of Athens fell into debt and was pressed for the money by his creditor; but he had no means of paying at the time, so he begged for a delay. But the creditor refused and said he must pay at once. Then the debtor fetched a sow – the only one he had – and took her to market to offer her for sale. It happened that his creditor was there too. Presently a buyer came along and asked if the sow produced good litters. 'Yes', said the debtor, 'very fine ones; and the remarkable thing is that she produces females at the Mysteries and males at the Panathenea'. (Festivals these were; and the Athenians always sacrifice a sow at one, and a boar at the other; while at the Dionysia they sacrifice a kid.) At that the creditor, who was standing by, put in, 'Don't be surprised, sir; why, still better, at the Dionysia this sow has kids!'

The Ass and His Masters

A gardener had an ass which had a very hard time of it, what with scanty food, heavy loads, and constant beating. The ass therefore begged Jupiter to take him away from the gardener and hand him over to another master. So Jupiter sent Mercury to the gardener to bid him sell the ass to a potter, which he did. But the ass was as discontented as ever, for he had to work harder than before: so he begged Jupiter for relief a second time, and Jupiter very obligingly arranged that he should be sold to a tanner. But when the ass saw what his new master's trade was, he cried in despair, 'Why wasn't I content to serve either of my former masters, hard as I had to work and badly as I was treated? For they would have buried me decently, but now I shall come in the end to the tanning vat'.

Servants don't know a good master till they have served a worse.

The Man and the Satyr

A man and a satyr became friends, and determined to live together. All went well for a while, until one day in winter-time the satyr saw the man blowing on his hands. 'Why do you do that?' he asked. 'To warm my hands', said the man. That same day, when they sat down to supper together, they each had a steaming hot bowl of porridge, and the man raised his bowl to his mouth and blew on it. 'Why do you do that?' asked the satyr. 'To cool my porridge', said the man. The satyr got up from the table. 'Good-bye', he said. 'I'm going: I can't be friends with a man who blows hot and cold with the same breath'.

The Cat and the Birds

A cat heard that the birds in an aviary were ailing. So he got himself up as a doctor, and, taking with him a set of the instruments proper to his profession, presented himself at the door, and inquired after the health of the birds. 'We shall do very well', they replied, without letting him in, 'when we've seen the last of you'.

A villain may disguise himself, but he will not deceive the wise.

ARackham 1912

The Viper and the File

A viper entered a carpenter's shop, and went from one to another of the tools, begging for something to eat. Among the rest, he addressed himself to the file, and asked for the favour of a meal. The file replied in a tone of pitying contempt, 'What a simpleton you must be if you imagine you will get anything from me, who invariably take from every one and never give anything in return'.

The covetous are poor givers.

The Crab and the Fox

A crab once left the sea-shore and went and settled in a meadow some way inland, which looked very nice and green and seemed likely to be a good place to feed in. But a hungry fox came along and spied the crab and caught him. Just as he was going to be eaten up, the crab said, 'This is just what I deserve; for I had no business to leave my natural home by the sea and settle here as though I belonged to the land'.

Be content with your lot.

The Father and His Daughters

A man had two daughters, one of whom he gave in marriage to a gardener, and the other to a potter. After a time he thought he would go and see how they were getting on; and first he went to the gardener's wife. He asked her how she was, and how things were going with herself and her husband. She replied that on the whole they were doing very well: 'But,' she continued, 'I do wish we could have some very good heavy rain: the garden wants it badly'. Then he went on to the potter's wife and made the same inquiries of her. She replied that she and her husband had nothing to complain of: 'But', she went on, 'I do wish we could have some nice dry weather, to dry the pottery'. Her father looked at her with a humorous expression on her face. 'You want dry weather', he said, 'and your sister wants rain. I was going to ask in my prayers that your wishes should be granted; but now it strikes me I had better not refer to the subject'.

The Wolf and the Goat

A wolf caught sight of a goat browsing above him on the scanty herbage that grew on the top of a steep rock; and being unable to get at her, tried to induce her to come lower down. 'You are risking your life up there, madam, indeed you are', he called out: 'pray take my advice and come down here, where you will find plenty of better food'. The goat turned a knowing eye upon him. 'It's little you care whether I get good grass or bad', said she: 'what you want is to eat me'.

The Bald Huntsman

A man who had lost all his hair took to wearing a wig, and one day he went out hunting. It was blowing rather hard at the time, and he hadn't gone far before a gust of wind caught his hat and carried it off, and his wig too, much to the amusement of the hunt. But he quite entered into the joke, and said, 'Ah, well! The hair that wig is made of didn't stick to the head on which it grew; so it's no wonder it won't stick to mine'.

The Horse and the Ass

A horse, proud of his fine harness, met an ass on the high-road. As the ass with his heavy burden moved slowly out of the way to let him pass, the horse cried out impatiently that he could hardly resist kicking him to make him move faster. The ass held his peace, but did not forget the other's insolence. Not long afterwards the horse became broken-winded, and was sold by his owner to a farmer. One day, as he was drawing a dung-cart, he met the ass again, who in turn derided him and said, 'Aha! you never thought to come to this, did you, you who were so proud! Where are all your gay trappings now?

The Owl and the Birds

The owl is a very wise bird; and once, long ago, when the first oak sprouted in the forest, she called all the other birds together and said to them, 'You see this tiny tree? If you take my advice, you will destroy it now when it is small: for when it grows big, the mistletoe will appear upon it, from which birdlime will be prepared for your destruction'. Again, when the first flax was sown, she said to them, 'Go and eat up that seed, for it is the seed of the flax, out of which men will one day make nets to catch you'. Once more, when she saw the first archer, she warned the birds that he was their deadly enemy, who would wing his arrows with their own feathers and shoot them. But they took no notice of what she said: in fact, they thought she was rather mad, and laughed at her. When, however, everything turned out as she had foretold, they changed their minds and conceived a great respect for her wisdom. Hence, whenever she appears, the birds attend upon her in the hope of hearing something that may be for their good. She, however, gives them advice no longer, but sits moping and pondering on the folly of her kind.

The Eagle and the Arrow

An eagle sat perched on a lofty rock, keeping a sharp look-out for prey. A huntsman, concealed in a cleft of the mountain and on the watch for game, spied him there and shot an arrow at him. The shaft struck him full in the breast and pierced him through and through. As he lay in the agonies of death, he turned his eyes upon the arrow. 'Ah! cruel fate!' he cried, 'that I should perish thus: but oh! fate more cruel still, that the arrow which kills me should be winged with an eagle's feathers'.

The Old Woman and the Wine-Jar

An old woman picked up an empty wine-jar which had once contained a rare and costly wine, and which still retained some traces of its exquisite bouquet. She raised it to her nose and sniffed at it again and again. 'Ah', she cried, 'how delicious must have been the liquid which has left behind so ravishing a smell'.

The Astronomer

There was once an astronomer whose habit it was to go out at night and observe the stars. One night, as he was walking about outside the town gates, gazing up absorbed into the sky and not looking where he was going, he fell into a dry well. As he lay there groaning, some one passing by heard him, and, coming to the edge of the well, looked down and, on learning what had happened, said, 'If you really mean to say that you were looking so hard at the sky that you didn't even see where your feet were carrying you along the ground, it appears to me that you deserve all you've got'.

Hercules and the Waggoner

A waggoner was driving his team along a muddy lane with a full load behind them, when the wheels of his waggon sank so deep in the mire that no efforts of his horses could move them. As he stood there, looking helplessly on, and calling loudly upon Hercules for assistance, the god himself appeared, and said to him, 'Put your shoulder to the wheel, man, and goad on your horses, and then you may call on Hercules to assist you. If you won't lift a finger to help yourself, you can't expect Hercules or any one else to come to your aid.

Heaven helps those who helps themselves.

The Wolf, the Mother, and Her Child

A hungry wolf was prowling about in search of food. By and by, attracted by the cries of a child, he came to a cottage. As he crouched beneath the window, he heard the mother say to the child, 'Stop crying, do! or I'll throw you to the wolf'. Thinking she really meant what she said, he waited there a long time in the expectation of satisfying his hunger. In the evening he heard the mother fondling her child and saying, 'If the naughty wolf comes, he shan't get my little one: Daddy will kill him'. The wolf got up in much disgust and walked away. 'As for the people in that house', said he to himself, 'you can't believe a word they say'.

The Town Mouse and the Country Mouse

A town mouse and a country mouse were acquaintances, and the country mouse one day invited his friend to come and see him at his home in the fields. The town mouse came, and they sat down to a dinner of barleycorns and roots, the latter of which had a distinctly earthy flavour. The fare was not much to the taste of the guest, and presently he broke out with 'My poor dear friend, you live here no better than the ants. Now, you should just see how I fare! My larder

is a regular horn of plenty. You must come and stay with me, and I promise you you shall live on the fat of the land'. So when he returned to town he took the country mouse with him, and showed him into a larder containing flour and oatmeal and figs and honey and dates. The country mouse had never seen anything like it, and sat down to enjoy the luxuries his friend provided: but before they had well begun, the door of the larder opened and someone came in. The two mice scampered off and hid themselves in a narrow and exceedingly uncomfortable hole. Presently, when all was quiet, they ventured out again; but someone else came in, and off they scuttled again. This was too much for the visitor. 'Good-bye', said he, 'I'm off. You live in the lap of luxury, I see, but you are surrounded by dangers; whereas at home I can enjoy my simple dinner of roots and corns in peace'.

The Man and the Image

A poor man had a wooden image of a god, to which he used to pray daily for riches. He did this for a long time, but remained as poor as ever, till one day he caught up the image in disgust and hurled it with all his strength against the wall. The force of the blow split open the head and a quantity of gold coins fell out upon the floor. The man gathered them up greedily, and said, 'O you old fraud, you! When I honoured you, you did me no good whatsoever: but no sooner do I treat you to insults and violence than you make a rich man of me!'

The Lioness and the Vixen

A lioness and a vixen were talking together about their young, as mothers will, and saying how healthy and well-grown they were, and what beautiful coats they had, and how they were the image of their parents. 'My litter of cubs is a joy to see', said the fox; and then she added, rather maliciously, 'But I notice you never have more than one'. 'No', said the lioness grimly, 'but that one's a lion'.

Quality, not quantity.

The Ass and the Mule

A certain man who had an ass and a mule loaded them both up one day and set out upon a journey. So long as the road was fairly level, the ass got on very well: but by and by they came to a place among the hills where the road was very rough and steep, and the ass was at his last gasp. So he begged the mule to relieve him of a part of his load: but the mule refused. At last, from sheer

weariness, the ass stumbled and fell down a steep place and was killed. The driver was in despair, but he did the best he could: he added the ass's load to the mule's, and he also flayed the ass and put his skin on the top of the double load. The mule could only just manage the extra weight, and, as he staggered painfully along, he said to himself, 'I have only got what I deserved: if I had been willing to help the ass at first, I should not now be carrying the load and his skin into the bargain'.

The Trumpeter Taken Prisoner

A trumpeter marched into battle in the van of the army and put courage into his comrades by his warlike tunes. Being captured by the enemy, he begged for his life, and said, 'Do not put me to death; I have killed no one; indeed, I have no weapons, but carry with me only my trumpet here'. But his captors replied, 'That is only the more reason why we should take your life; for, though you do not fight yourself, you stir up others to do so'.

The Goatherd and the Goat

A goatherd was one day gathering his flock to return to the fold, when one of his goats strayed and refused to join the rest. He tried for a long time to get her to return by calling and whistling to her, but the goat took no notice of him at all; so at last he threw a stone at her and broke one of her horns. In dismay, he begged her not to tell his master: but she replied, 'You silly fellow, my horn would cry aloud even if I held my tongue'.

It's no use trying to hide what can't be hidden.

The Traveller and Fortune

A traveller, exhausted with fatigue after a long journey, sank down at the very brink of a deep well and presently fell asleep. He was within an ace of falling in, when Dame Fortune appeared to him and touched him on the shoulder, cautioning him to move further away. 'Wake up, good sir, I pray you', she said; 'had you fallen into the well, the blame would have been thrown not on your own folly but on me, Fortune'.

The Woman and the Farmer

A woman, who had lately lost her husband, used to go every day to his grave and lament her loss. A farmer, who was engaged in ploughing not far from the spot, set eyes upon the woman and desired to have her for his wife; so he left his plough and came and sat by her side, and began to shed tears himself. She asked him why he wept; and he replied, 'I have lately lost my wife, who was very dear to me, and tears ease my grief'. 'And I', said she, 'have lost my husband'. And so for a while they mourned in silence. Then he said, 'Since you and I are in like case, shall we not do well to marry and live together? I shall take the place of your dead husband, and you, that of my dead wife'. The woman consented to the plan, which indeed seemed reasonable enough; and they dried their tears. Meanwhile, a thief had come and stolen the oxen which the farmer had left with his plough. On discovering the theft, he beat his breast and loudly bewailed his loss. When the woman heard his cries, she came and said, 'Why, are you weeping still?' To which he replied, 'Yes, and I mean it this time'.

Prometheus and the Making of Man

At the bidding of Jupiter, Prometheus set about the creation of man and the other animals. Jupiter, seeing that mankind, the only rational creatures, were far outnumbered by the irrational beasts, bade him redress the balance by turning some of the latter into men. Prometheus did as he was bidden, and this is the reason why some people have the forms of men but the souls of beasts.

The Swallow and the Crow

A swallow was once boasting to a crow about her birth. 'I was once a princess', said she, 'the daughter of a king of Athens, but my husband used me cruelly, and cut out my tongue for a slight fault. Then, to protect me from further injury, I was turned by Juno into a bird'. 'You chatter quite enough as it is', said the crow. 'What you would have been like if you hadn't lost your tongue, I can't think'.

The Bear and the Fox

A bear was once bragging about his generous feelings, and saying how refined he was compared with other animals. (There is, in fact, a tradition that a bear will never touch a dead body.) A fox, who heard him talking in this strain, smiled and said, 'My friend, when you are hungry, I only wish you would confine your attention to the dead and leave the living alone'.

A hypocrite deceives no one but himself.

The Fowler, the Partridge and the Cock

One day, as a fowler was sitting down to a scanty supper of herbs and bread, a friend dropped in unexpectedly. The larder was empty; so he went out and caught a tame partridge, which he kept as a decoy, and was about to wring her neck when she cried, 'Surely you won't kill me? Why, what will you do without me next time you go fowling? How will you get the birds to come to your nets?' He let her go at this, and went to his hen-house, where he had a plump young cock. When the cock saw what he was after, he too pleaded for his life, and said, 'If you kill me, how will you know the time of night? And who will wake you up in the morning when it is time to get to work?' The fowler, however, replied, 'You are useful for telling the time, I know; but, for all that, I can't send my friend supperless to bed'. And therewith he caught him and wrung his neck.

The Trees and the Axe

A woodman went into the forest and begged of the trees the favour of a handle for his axe. The principal trees at once agreed to so modest a request, and unhesitatingly gave him a young ash sapling, out of which he fashioned the handle he desired. No sooner had he done so than he set to work to fell the noblest trees in the wood. When they saw the use to which he was putting their gift, they cried, 'Alas! alas! We are undone, but we are ourselves to blame. The little we gave has cost us all: had we not sacrificed the rights of the ash, we might ourselves have stood for ages'.

The Bald Man and the Fly

A fly settled on the head of a bald man and bit him. In his eagerness to kill it, he hit himself a smart slap. But the fly escaped, and said to him in derision, 'You tried to kill me for just one little bite; what will you do to yourself now, for the heavy smack you have just given yourself?' 'Oh, for the blow I bear no grudge', he replied, 'for I never intended myself any harm; but as for you, you contemptible insect, who live by sucking human blood, I'd have borne a good deal more than that for the satisfaction of dashing the life out of you!'

The Dog and the Cook

A rich man once invited a number of friends and acquaintances to a banquet. His dog thought it would be a good opportunity to invite another dog, a friend of his; so he went to him and said, 'My master is giving a feast: there'll be a fine spread, so come and dine with me tonight'. The dog thus invited came, and when he saw the preparations being made in the kitchen he said to himself, 'My word, I'm in luck: I'll take care to eat enough tonight to last me two or three days'. At the same time he wagged his tail briskly, by way of showing his friend how delighted he was to have been asked. But just then the cook caught sight of him, and, in his annoyance at seeing a strange dog in the kitchen, caught him up by the hind legs and threw him out of the window. He had a nasty fall, and limped away as quickly as he could, howling dismally. Presently some other dogs met him, and said, 'Well, what sort of a dinner did you get?' To which he replied, 'I had a splendid time: the wine was so good, and I drank so much of it, that I really don't remember how I got out of the house!'

Be shy of favours bestowed at the expense of others.

The Mule

One morning a mule, who had too much to eat and too little to do, began to think himself a very fine fellow indeed, and frisked about saying, 'My father was undoubtedly a high-spirited horse and I take after him entirely'. But very soon afterwards he was put into the harness and compelled to go a very long way with a heavy load behind him. At the end of the day, exhausted by his unusual exertions, he said dejectedly to himself, 'I must have been mistaken about my father; he can only have been an ass after all'.